Weird Files - The Alien Science Bus

Written by:
Derek Keilty

Illustrated by Charlie Clough

First Published
April 08 in Great Britain by

ISBN-10: 1-905637-46-2
ISBN-13: 978-1-905637-46-1

Contents

"For my twin daughters, Sarah-Jane and Rebekah,
who were first to board the science bus."

About Me

My name is Danny Weir but most of the kids at my school call me Danny Weird. Stupid isn't it . . . just because you're a bit different, people make up names? Anyway I don't let it bother me. There are good things about being different as well.

So how am I different? I'll tell you. First, there's the fact that electric things go wonky when I touch them. Everybody knows to keep me away from their TV's, computer games and mobile phones. I can't wear watches and the clock radio in my bedroom never keeps the right time. I even had to build my own 'Danny proof' computer as my old one kept crashing when I touched it. (I love science and electronic stuff but I've had to learn to do things my way.) My mum told me my pram was struck by lightening when I was a baby. Maybe that's the reason. Or maybe there is another reason I don't know about.

But there's another secret side of me that nobody really knows about, not even my mum or dad or my best friends. I have these special powers! Quite a long time ago, I discovered I had a kind of weird sense for detecting anything extra-terrestrial or paranormal. I can see things like ectoplasm and extraplasm - the green, slimy stuff aliens and paranormal beings sometimes leave behind them, which other people would never see. And where other people just see something ordinary I can see where there's something alien or paranormal hiding beneath the surface.

What's really odd is that since I discovered I had this weird sense, weird stuff seems to follow me around like a stray dog. So now I keep a file every time something weird happens, every time I even hear of something weird happening. I have a database of hundreds of files and it's growing all the time and it's now a part of the 'WWWW' or 'World Wide Weird Web'. No one would believe it could have been created by an ordinary ten year old boy - there's some really amazing stuff.

For instance, this is the file I opened the day the Science Bus visited my school . . .

Greenman Primary School

Monday, 9am

I'd walked into school thinking it was going to be a normal Monday. Then I saw it, parked in the playground.

'The Science Bus!' I said out loud. It came every year but I'd totally forgotten it was coming this week. I couldn't wait to get on the bus. We had to go in small groups and it seemed like years before my teacher Miss

Fish announced, 'Okay, Danny, Will and Luke off you go.'

Luke and Will made a screwed up face. They weren't the least bit interested in Science or even school. I often wondered how we had ever become friends.

'You're weird for wanting to learn about Science,' Luke sneered as soon as we left the classroom. 'It's so boring!'

I looked him up and down, grinning. 'Least I don't look like an experiment that went wrong.'

Will sniggered and Luke elbowed him.

I expected it to be the same teacher as last year but a skinny, black-haired man with a stern face and glasses, stood at the door of the bus.

'Welcome aboard, I'm Mr Allen,' he said in a deep voice.

We had only just boarded the bus when disaster struck. Luke tripped on a mat and knocked over the solar system display. The Earth along with Venus, Mars, and Mercury all went rolling around the bus floor. Mr Allen didn't look very pleased.

'Watch where you're going!' he shouted. 'Now hurry and pick them all up before they get lost.'

I grabbed Venus and Mercury while Will dribbled the Earth like a football. Luke posed with a red planet under his heel. 'Hey look at me, first boy to set foot on the moon!'

'That's Mars,' I said.

'Stop messing about and pass them to me!'

Mr Allen stuck the polystyrene planets back onto what looked like knitting needles. Strangely though, he mixed some of them up. And that's when my weird sense kicked in. I felt the hairs on my neck stand up and a tingly feeling run up and down my spine. The next thing, I noticed his eyes turn a funny lizard green colour. He caught my eye.

'Well?' he frowned.

'Er, I think you need to swap Mercury and Earth around.'

Mr Allen gave me a funny smile. 'Of course I do, just testing to see if you were paying attention,' he said, switching them back. 'Well now let's make a start. First we'll look at forces, with an experiment about wind power.'

Will sniggered. 'I know how to make great wind power . . . eat the beans in school dinners!'

I smiled at Will's joke, but couldn't believe my ears when Luke whispered.

'Look at all those batteries, millions of them. I could do with some o' them for my PSP.'

Even Will looked shocked. 'You can't just help yourself, Luke,' he hissed.

'We could play it at lunchtime.'

'I don't know, what if we get caught?'

'Boys that's enough chatter,' said Mr Allen, 'now who'll help me by holding this balloon?'

I put up my hand but Luke almost snatched the balloon out of Mr Allen's hand.

'I'll do it!'

'Watch you don't take off,' said Will.

I imagined Luke drifting up to the bus roof hanging by the balloon string and grinned.

'Now hold tight till I fix on this piece of plastic tubing, then we'll attach it to our little boat,' said Mr Allen.

Luke's nose wrinkled. 'I think I'm going to sneeze!'

'Don't let go of that balloon!'

'Don't worry, I . . . A . . . A . . . Atishoo! Oh no!'

The balloon shot off around the bus, tipping over a small ant farm, knocking down a cardboard skeleton and skimming across a tray of water until it slapped like a wet fish

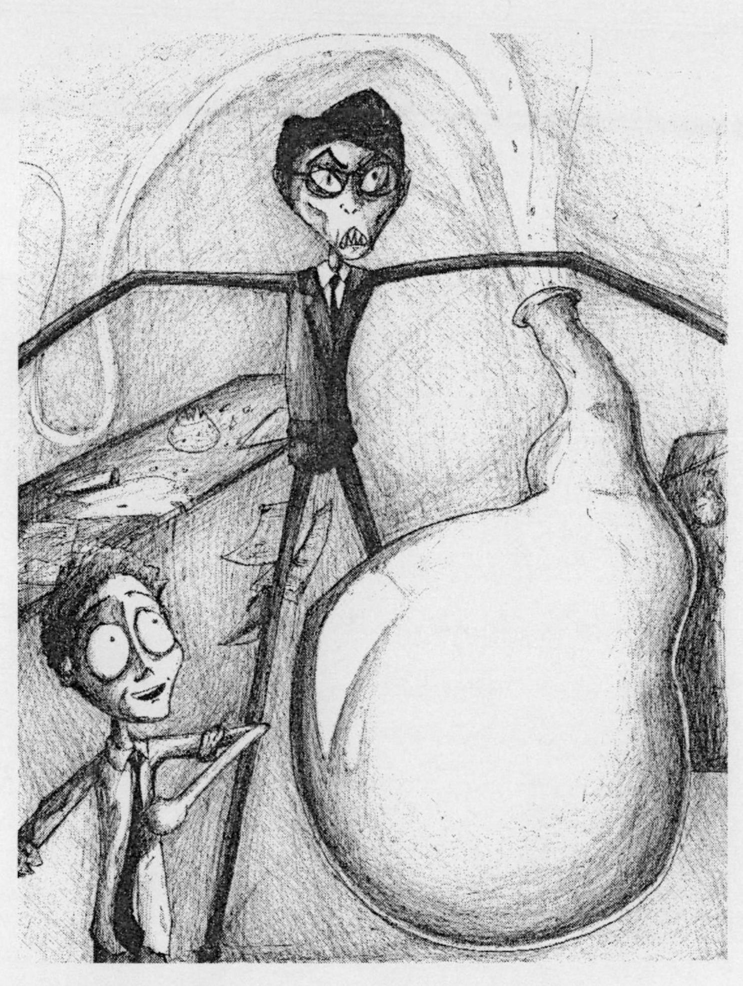

right into Mr Allen's face.

Mr Allen looked annoyed. I noticed his eyes turn green and lizardy again. Luke and Will tried desperately not to laugh but that just made it worse.

I began picking up the skeleton bones till I noticed something crawling on the floor.

'Look!' I said, pointing to the ant farm that had tipped over, 'the ants are escaping!'

Mr Allen was fuming. 'Oh for pity's sake, this is all we need. Listen you lot, you'll have to wait outside for a few minutes,' he ordered.

'Can I help?' I asked.

'No, I think you've all done enough for now.'

We jumped off the bus. I was annoyed at Luke. 'This is your fault. We've only got half an hour to go round.'

Luke fiddled with his PSP, which was making wonky noises, as the batteries were good as done. 'Humph, who cares?'

'There's something odd about him. Did you see his eyes when he got mad?' I said.

'Nope.'

They both looked at me as if I'd gone bonkers. I needed to see what Mr Allen was up to. 'Hey Will, give us a leg up will you?'

Will cupped his hands and lifted me up to the bus window. I peeked inside. It was hard to see through the smoky glass but I could just make out Mr Allen setting the ant farm back onto the table. It looked empty.

'I think all the ants have escaped!' I

said, squinting to try and see a bit better. Mr Allen suddenly slammed the table with his hand. I grinned. 'Well, not quite all of them.'

Then I stared in disbelief. Mr Allen lifted the squished ant and popped it into his mouth. Then another – and another, licking his lips with a ghastly green tongue, which was forked - like a snake's tongue.

'What is it?' said Will.

'I . . . I think I just saw Mr Allen eat a mouthful of ants.'

A second later Mr Allen stuck his head out the door. 'Get down from there. I don't want any more accidents,' he roared.

'Sorry Sir.'

Mr Allen gave me a stare that sent my weird sense racing. 'Right now, you can all come back aboard.'

Inside I looked at the ant farm. It was completely empty. Mr Allen was still chewing.

'What are you eating?' I plucked up the courage to ask.

'Jellybeans. Someone from the last

group must've left them,' he said.

Since when do jellybeans move, I thought? That did it; it was time to open a weird file on Mr Allen.

School Corridor

Monday 12:05pm

At lunch I found a quiet spot and took out my mobile phone. It was more than just an ordinary mobile. The front flipped open to reveal a powerful palm computer. I'd put it together myself using an old, out-dated mobile and some other electronics. (I'd added special insulation to make it Danny-proof.)

I typed in my password and a second later a big green W filled the screen. I'd accessed the Weird Files.

```
Create New File
View/Edit Files
Browse Weird Archive
Surf WWWW (World Wide Weird Web)
```

I pressed N and opened a new weird file on Mr Allen, typing in the morning's events.

When I'd finished, the computer scanned the archive, comparing hundreds of weird files with the file I'd just created. It displayed some files it thought might be of interest. One in particular surprised me - it was something I remembered investigating last year, just a few miles away from here, but I couldn't think what it could really have to do with Mr Allen.

I clicked on it.

Greenman, England, 2007

Darwin Mudd, a farmer, stopped his tractor in the middle of a field to take a break when he saw a flying saucer emerge from the fog. It hovered for a few seconds, shining a blindingly bright beam of light at him. Then it shot off at high speed. He reported it to his local paper. Certain others in the area would have spotted it too, but there were no further reports . . .

'I'd be careful not to let that out of my sight,' said a voice behind me. I whirled round, instantly closing the phone.

It was Mr Allen. I froze. I'd have to go back to the Farmer Mudd file later.

'Must've cost a small fortune,' he grinned. 'What are you doing?'

'Eh n . . . nothing,' I stuttered.

'I love technology stuff. Can I have a look?'

It was the worst possible question, he could've asked me. If he knew what I'd been doing then . . . he took it off me!!

'I won't damage it.'

As he held it I noticed his fingernails had an unusual green glow to them and underneath I saw, just for a moment, a ripple of scales. His fingers seemed suddenly far too thin. They curled round the phone like a grotesque skinny ghost spider, flipping it open.

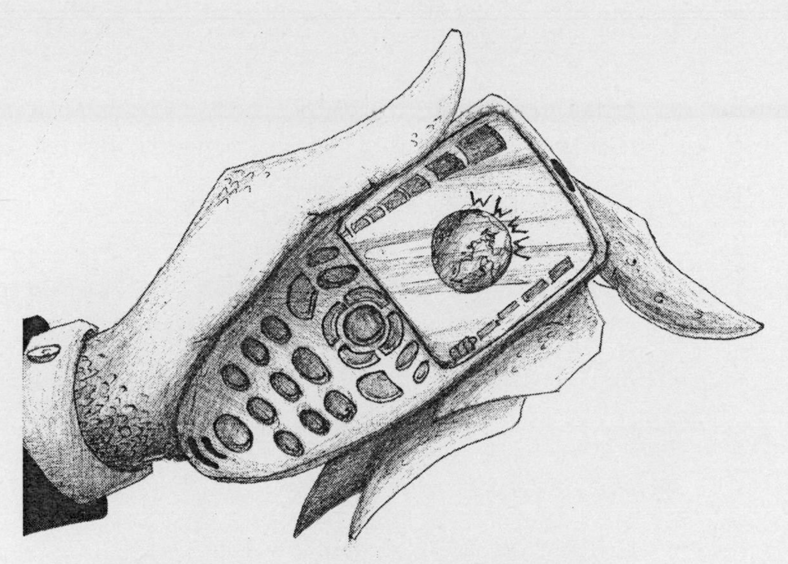

He saw me staring and grinned. 'Amazing!'

He put his hand on my shoulder and suddenly probably the weirdest thing that had ever happened to me happened. He spoke to me inside my mind.

Well now, what have we here? You can hear me, can't you Danny?

I found myself answering him in my

head. *Yes. Yes, I can hear you.*

I'm impressed. And there's me thinking human beings were really rather basic creatures.

Who are you?

Ah, questions, questions - undoubtedly why you humans have come so far . . .

Suddenly the bell rang. I gasped with relief.

'I have to go, Sir.'

He handed me back my phone. 'On you go. And careful with that phone, eh?'

My House

Monday 3.30pm

Pyrogovkoye Lake, Russia.

Vladimir Kranksky while out fishing noticed an oval-shaped object in the sky. Later two small men approached him. They put their spindly arms, which were twice as long as human arms, on his forehead and spoke to him telepathically. They asked him where they might find the ruling species of Planet Earth. When Kranksky explained that he was a human being and that human beings were the ruling species, the aliens seemed to bleat (like a sort of laughter). Then one of them took out a picture of a dolphin. Kranksky explained that dolphins weren't the ruling species but were friendly mammals that lived in the sea, at which point the aliens seemed to get a bit cross and stormed off. He never saw them again . . .

I'd gone home and was sitting in the living room looking up stuff about touch telepathy on the World Wide Weird Web.

'Oh not the TV now!'

I looked up from my mobile screen and saw that Mum had come into the living room and looked very cross. The TV screen was flickering and making an awful hissing noise.

'Must've come on itself. I wasn't watching it.'

'Oh Danny,' she scolded, pointing the remote at the snowy screen, 'what has Dad told you about touching the TV?'

'I . . . I didn't touch it, honest,' I protested.

Mum pushed in the button on the TV set. The screen flickered then the picture came back as normal.

'See, I didn't break it.'

'No, but you've broken the remote,' Mum

sighed. 'To add to the three clock radios, the microwave, not to mention my laptop . . . and I'm still paying for it!'

Shoving my mobile in my pocket, I shuffled outside to the garage. The pull-up garage door was half up and I crouched down and went inside. Dad was stooped over the bonnet of an old Mini he'd bought for a few hundred pounds at an auction.

'How was the Science Bus?' Dad asked.

'Different,' I nodded to the car. 'What's wrong with it?'

'Electrical faults for one thing an' finding them is like looking for a needle in a haystack.'

I went to lean on the bonnet but Dad dived in front of me. 'Don't touch anything!'

'Wha . . . oh sorry, I forgot.'

I looked up and saw two pairs of feet below the garage door. I lifted the door. It was Luke and Will holding their skateboards.

'We're taking our decks up the high street. Coming?'

I wasn't really in the mood. 'Dunno.'

'C'mon,' Will coaxed.

Five minutes later we were doing kick-flips at the fountain in the high street. Will liked an audience - though not when he fell on his bum.

We hadn't been skateboarding long when out of the crowd who should appear but Mr Allen. He seemed to be everywhere.

He didn't notice us. I watched him make a beeline for the pet shop.

'Isn't that the Science Bus teacher?' Will commented.

I stared. 'He's no teacher!'

'Bus driver then or whatever?'

I skated over to get a better view. 'He's nothing from this world. Didn't you think he was acting a bit strange on the Science Bus?'

Will shook his head.

'All teachers are strange,' said Luke.

Mr Allen had gone into the pet shop. I peered through the window, trying to catch a glimpse of him, but all I saw were baby rabbits twitching their noses at me.

'Let's go in and see what he's up to,' I said.

'I'm not,' Luke groaned. 'What's the big deal anyway?'

'I'll go,' said Will.

Luke sighed, following us into the shop. Inside we kept out of sight, pretending to look at the tropical fish.

'Can you see what he's doing?'

'I think he's buying a cage,' said Will.

Luke rolled his eyes 'Call the cops.'

I squinted through a shelf full of dog food. 'It's a mouse cage, look he's buying mice.' I frowned. 'Wow! He's buying loads of them.'

'That's weird; most people only buy one or two. What's he up to?' said Will.

'I don't know but I'm gonna find out. C'mon, we'll follow him.'

We went back outside and waited. A minute later Mr Allen appeared, carrying the mouse cage, half covered with a bag.

We let him walk up the street a bit before I lifted my deck. 'C'mon!'

But Will froze.

'What's the matter?'

'S . . . S . . . Snakes!' Will pointed.

Slithering out of the pet shop door were at least six snakes, their tongues flickering. They were nearly a metre long

OLI'S
PETS

with red, yellow and black rings round their slimy bodies.

'They look poisonous! What sort of pets is that shop selling?' I said.

No one except us seemed to notice the snakes as they split up and disappeared into holes and gutters along the road.

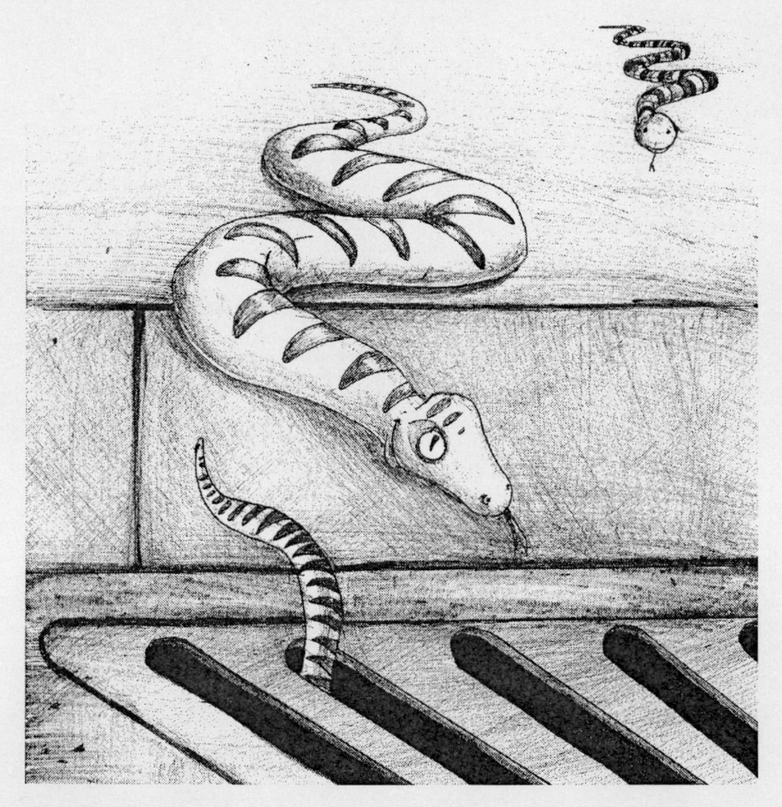

But the snakes weren't the only things slithering away.

'Never mind the snakes, Mr Allen's getting away, c'mon.'

'D'ya think he did that?' Will asked as we hurried after him.

'I'm sure he did.'

We ran up the street but couldn't see him anywhere.

'The entry,' I shouted and we doubled back, 'and watch you don't get bitten by those snakes.'

Running down an alley to the town car park, we arrived just as the Science Bus was pulling away.

'He's gone.'

Will sighed. 'And the snakes too . . .'

Luke and Will wanted to go on to the park and carry on with skateboarding.

I headed back to the pet shop. But, by the time I got back, a 'shop closed' sign was already swinging on the door. I suppose I wasn't that surprised. The shop owner was probably frantically searching for his missing deadly reptiles.

I was skating for home when my phone rang. It was Farmer Mudd.

Was it just a coincidence? It must've been a year since I talked to him. 'That's funny,' I told him, 'I was just reading about you today.'

He sounded worried, 'Can yer come over for half an hour? I've somethin' you might be interested in.'

Mudd Farm

Monday, 5.45pm

'I weren't gonna ring, y'know, but somethin' weird's happened again.'

We were sitting in a smelly old barn, surrounded by bales of hay.

Farmer Mudd's eye twitched nervously and every now and then he got up to peer out of the window.

'Folk round 'ere still thinks I'm mad. Last month some pranksters dressed up one o' my scarecrows to look like an alien. Sprayed him silver and stuck two little antennas on his head.'

I stifled a chuckle then felt a bit guilty. Farmer Mudd looked very serious.

'Anyway, I thought I'd tell you an' no one else. As long as you keeps it to yourself mind?'

I nodded expectantly. 'Course, what's happened?'

He breathed a deep sigh. 'I saw it again. A spaceship like the last one, only this time it nearly took my head off. Came skimmin' across the field one evenin', like an oval shape . . . grey with dim lights - I'm sure it was the same ship.'

'Don't suppose you'd time to get a picture?'

He shook his head. 'I barely had time to see, it were travellin' so fast. Then it seemed to slow down, almost like it were descending. I drove round for days keepin' an eye out but nothin'.'

Mrs Mudd brought a tray of tea in and I saw her give her husband a worried look. Obviously even she didn't believe him.

He slurped his tea. 'An' that's not all.'

I peered at him over my mug. 'It's not?'

'Bring yer tea.'

We left the barn and walked over to the old farmhouse. Inside Mrs Mudd sat by a roaring fire and I followed Farmer Mudd up two flights of creaky wooden stairs to an attic room.

He waved me over to the window. 'Have a look out there.'

In the centre of a golden field, the corn had been flattened in the shape of a perfect circle.

'A crop circle - wow that's huge!' I said out loud. It was the first time I'd seen one in real life.

'Appeared yesterday, just two days after I saw the ship.'

'Amazing. Can I take a closer look?'

Minutes later we were standing in the middle of the crop circle. I could feel my weird sense prickle the back of my neck.

'This is mega, a real phenomenon. It must mean there's extra-terrestrial activity in this area and I'll bet Mr Allen has something to do with it.'

Farmer Mudd frowned. 'Who's Mr Allen?'

I told him about our creepy Science Bus

teacher, about his ant eating, scaly fingernails and soft spot for mice and snakes.

Farmer Mudd's eyebrows crept further up his forehead. He looked in his mug. 'I think we both need a refill.'

My Room

Monday 9.30 pm

I lay on top of my bed. It had been quite a day but one thing was bugging me. If Mr Allen was an extra-terrestrial or something as I suspected, there should've been traces of extraplasm in the Science Bus. My phone was on the bed and I flipped it open logging onto the World Wide Weird Web. I typed 'alien disguises' into the search engine.

Alien disguises can take a whole variety of forms, though usually they don't bother. Where infiltration is necessary there have been accounts of aliens using quite sophisticated human disguises, some using a process called hypnotic projection while others use a simpler process known as plain old dressing up.
Hyper intelligent aliens are known to possess the ability to morph themselves into many terrestrial forms both animal and human. There is an account of one alien who on a visit to earth took the form of a pot of flowers, sending data back to his home planet from the window box of a Miss Florence Winterbottom's top floor apartment.

I wasn't sure when I fell asleep but I had a totally weird dream about being abducted by a giant daffodil.

School Library

Tuesday 10:30am

Next day in the library, I was heading to the Science section, when a big T-Rex jumped in front of my eyes.

'Rooooaarr!'

I pushed the dinosaur book away from my face only to see another big lizard holding it.

'Very funny Luke,' I smirked.

'Ugh! Science again. I'm getting this one,' Luke proudly announced. 'Look, it's got a tape of dino noises.'

I didn't look. Something Miss Fish was reading had caught my eye. It was a newspaper headline.

OLI'S PET SHOP CLOSED DOWN FOR SELLING EXOTIC PETS - INCLUDING POISONOUS SNAKES.

I tugged Luke's sleeve. 'Those snakes in the pet shop - they were poisonous. It's in the paper.'

Luke's mouth dropped open and he clutched his throat. 'Uggh! I could've been bitten by a poisonous snake!'

I felt my weird sense tingle and looked around to see Mr Allen walk into the library and take a seat at one of the computers. He logged onto the Internet and placed a peculiar looking disc into the CD Rom drive.

It wasn't the usual silver colour but gold and glowing dimly. I drifted closer to see what he was up to.

I spotted Miss Fish look at me over the top rim of her glasses. 'Danny, remember you're not to touch the computer,' she said smiling.

I nodded. 'Is that a new type of CD Mr Allen?'

He shoved it in quickly as I spoke. 'Hello Danny, yes, told you I love technology stuff. Holds exabytes of info. How's that phone gadget of yours?'

'Oh I left it at home,' I fibbed. I didn't want him getting his scaly fingers on it a second time.

'Exabytes eh? You could download half the Internet onto that. Where'd you get it?'

'You wouldn't have heard of it, it's miles away from here . . .' He smiled that sneaky smile I was beginning to loathe.

While Miss Fish was busy reading the paper, I slipped off my shoe and touched the modem cable with my foot. The screen flickered then went blank.

'Oh dear, looks like the server's down, Sir,' I said trying to keep a straight face. He wouldn't be able to download anything now.

He banged the keyboard. 'Stupid thing!

I was right in the middle of something too.'

Miss Fish frowned at me. 'Danny.'

I showed her my hands were nowhere near it.

Mr Allen was staring at me suspiciously when Will wandered past. 'You got one yet?'

I smiled. 'I'd better go and pick a library book.'

School Canteen

Tuesday 12.15pm

I had just bitten into a tuna sandwich when my mobile bleeped telling me I had an e-mail. I opened and read it:

Danny,

I know who you are . . . keep your nose out of it - or else!

wwww.weirdsecrets/arch/file716.htm

I clicked on the weird web link and downloaded the web page.

Danny Weir.

Ten-year-old extra-terrestrial and paranormal intelligence collector/archivist and investigator, said to have assisted FBI and MI6 by allowing them access to his database of weird intelligence (finest in Britain). Rumours of his having special powers also exist. And his several attempts to block this weird website are perhaps proof there may be some truth in the rumours . . .

It had to be from Mr Allen. It was an entry from a weird website I'd had banned from the WWWW for displaying secret and sensitive data, not to mention the stuff about me. But they were obviously back in business and Mr Allen had been doing his homework on me on the web search engines.

School Playground

Tuesday 3.05pm

I had just begun crossing the playground when Will ran up to me panting furiously.

'Danny, it's Luke - he's been kidnapped by Mr Allen!'

'What?'

'He was trying to borrow some

batteries from the Science Bus. He told me to keep watch. Then as Luke's getting off, Mr Allen grabs him and drags him back on board, yelling.'

'Hang on. Hang on,' I said. 'When did this happen?'

'Just now.'

Will pointed to an upstairs window on the bus. 'I saw his face; he's taken him upstairs. He was calling for help. What are we gonna do?'

'And did you see Mr Allen upstairs too?'

'I think so!'

I started walking towards the door of the Science Bus, 'Right, c'mon!'

'Where?'

'On the bus of course. Where do you think?'

'He was so mad looking. What if he captures us too?'

'We can't just leave Luke in there.'

I hurried over to the door and sneaked aboard. Will followed me.

At the back of the bus, behind a curtain, were piles of books. Flipping one open, I gasped.

'What kind of language is this?'

'Never seen writing like it,' said Will.

'Look, I know you're probably going to think I'm nuts but I think Mr Allen could be . . .' I paused, picking up a pencil that lay nearby and wrote Mr Allen then I deliberately dotted the second 'L' .

Will gasped. 'Alien!' He drew back, losing his balance and fell against a cupboard that creaked and opened.

We both stared inside.

'The mice,' I gasped.

'Wow! What's he done to them?' said Will.

About ten mice were scurrying inside a cage. On their heads were tiny helmets with wires sticking out of them. And the wires seemed to be hooked up to an electronic device that hummed and printed out gobbledygook. At last, I noticed tiny traces of extraplasm on the outside of the cage. The first I'd seen.

Will poked his finger at them.

'Don't touch anything,' I warned him. 'Secret experiments, what next?' I'd have liked a closer look but my weird sense began rushing through my head. 'We need to think of a plan to rescue Luke from upstairs, quick.'

Suddenly I heard footsteps on the bus staircase. 'He's coming down!'

I peeked through the curtain. Mr Allen was striding down the bus stairs holding a green glass ball and muttering a strange gibberish. He strode up towards the front of the bus.

'What's he doing?' Will whispered.

'Looks like he's . . . talking to that green orb thing,' I frowned.

'Is that some kind of new mobile?'

PLEASE

'Never seen a mobile made of green glass,' I said.

Mr Allen sat down in the driver's seat and started the engine. We stared at each other, but before either of us could even think about making a run for it, the bus was on its way out of the playground.

Will gulped. 'We have to tell him we're on the bus,' he blubbed.

'Great and maybe you'd like to explain just what you were doing on the bus,' I said. 'Anyway, when was the last time you saw a grown-up talking to a green orb?'

'What are you saying Danny?'

'Like I said, I don't know who or what he is exactly but he's not Mr Allen.'

Somewhere in the Countryside

Tuesday 3.55pm

Finally, I felt the Science Bus stop. Will had hardly moved in the back.

I peered through a window. 'I think we're in the countryside somewhere,' I whispered.

I didn't dare breathe as Mr Allen went

upstairs. The next minute, Luke appeared, his hands tied behind his back like a prisoner. Mr Allen shoved him along, picking up some books before forcing him off the bus.

'What do we do now?' asked Will. 'Panic?'

'That won't help,' I replied, following Mr Allen off the bus. 'I'm *going* to see what he's up to.'

'Wait for me.'

Mr Allen had taken us to what looked like, a disused aircraft hangar, all rusted and with smashed windows. The countryside around looked familiar but there wasn't time to think about that right now. Trying to keep out of sight, I caught a *glimpse* of him closing a side door.

'He's gone in there. Come on!'

'I think we should get out of here,' said Will.

'And leave Luke to whatever Mr Allen has planned for him - great idea!'

I crept over to the hangar door, pushing it open slightly.

The door creaked and I froze. Behind me I heard Will dive into a bush. Still, I'd opened it just enough to see inside. And what I saw made me gasp.

The far end of the building looked like a cross between a lab and a gym. There were all sorts of gadgets on pulleys, trampolines, big tanks full of things, and tables full of test tubes, pipes and bubbling bottles of luminous liquids.

But that wasn't all. Squatting behind the apparatus, like a giant daddy long legs, its colourful lights winking on and off, stood a SPACESHIP.

I turned round slowly to see Will's face staring at me like a frightened animal in a bush.

'What is it?' he asked.

'It's . . . it's a spaceship,' I said in wonder.

Will choked. 'A spaceship! You're pulling my leg.'

I stepped back. 'See for yourself.'

Will peered in and gasped.

'It must be a model or something.'

'Looks pretty real to me.'

'Very observant, boy, that's because it is real!' said an angry voice nearby.

'Mr Allen!'

I stared at him, shaking my head. Mr Allen noticed and grinned. 'Ha, I knew you were the clever one!' And taking off his glasses he began tugging at his neck, which started to wrinkle and loosen.

'Well if that is a spaceship then that makes you . . . '

Will paused, watching as Mr Allen rolled up his face to reveal scaly green skin.

' . . . An alien!' Will finished, horrified.

'Brilliant!' said the alien. 'Now c'mon, get inside. I'm in a foul mood.'

Inside the Hangar

Tuesday 4.05pm

The alien pushed and shoved us inside the hangar, which reeked of the bubbling chemicals.

'You knew we were in the bus all the time, didn't you?' I said.

The alien strode to a table with racks of experiments on top of it and began twiddling dials and tapping test tubes. 'I'm not deaf y'know. You were making an unearthly racket. Then I got distracted by that stupid call from my home planet, telling me I should've been back days ago. Ungrateful morons! They've got no idea how hard I've been working . . . always said it was a huge task for one person but would they listen?'

'What task?' I asked.

'Testing your planet for colonisation,' said the alien calmly. 'I don't think they realise the half of what's involved y'know - hundreds of experiments, hours of reading, studying, analysing. It's exhausting. Anyway, that's where you come in.'

'Run out of mice have you?' I scowled.

He grinned and ran a bony finger under my chin. 'You're a clever little thing, aren't you? You probably know then that they're almost human - in terms of DNA that is.'

'Why'd you let the coral snakes go?' I asked.

'Felt sorry for them cooped up in those tiny cages. I like to think of them as my reptile cousins. And looks like pretty soon we reptoids will once again rule this little planet - just like the dinosaurs millions of years ago.'

The alien had tied Luke up to what looked like a giant battery, with loads of wires sticking out of it. Both his arms and feet were hooked up to some scary looking bits of metal.

'Anyway, Luke here's been very keen to help me with my recycling experiments.'

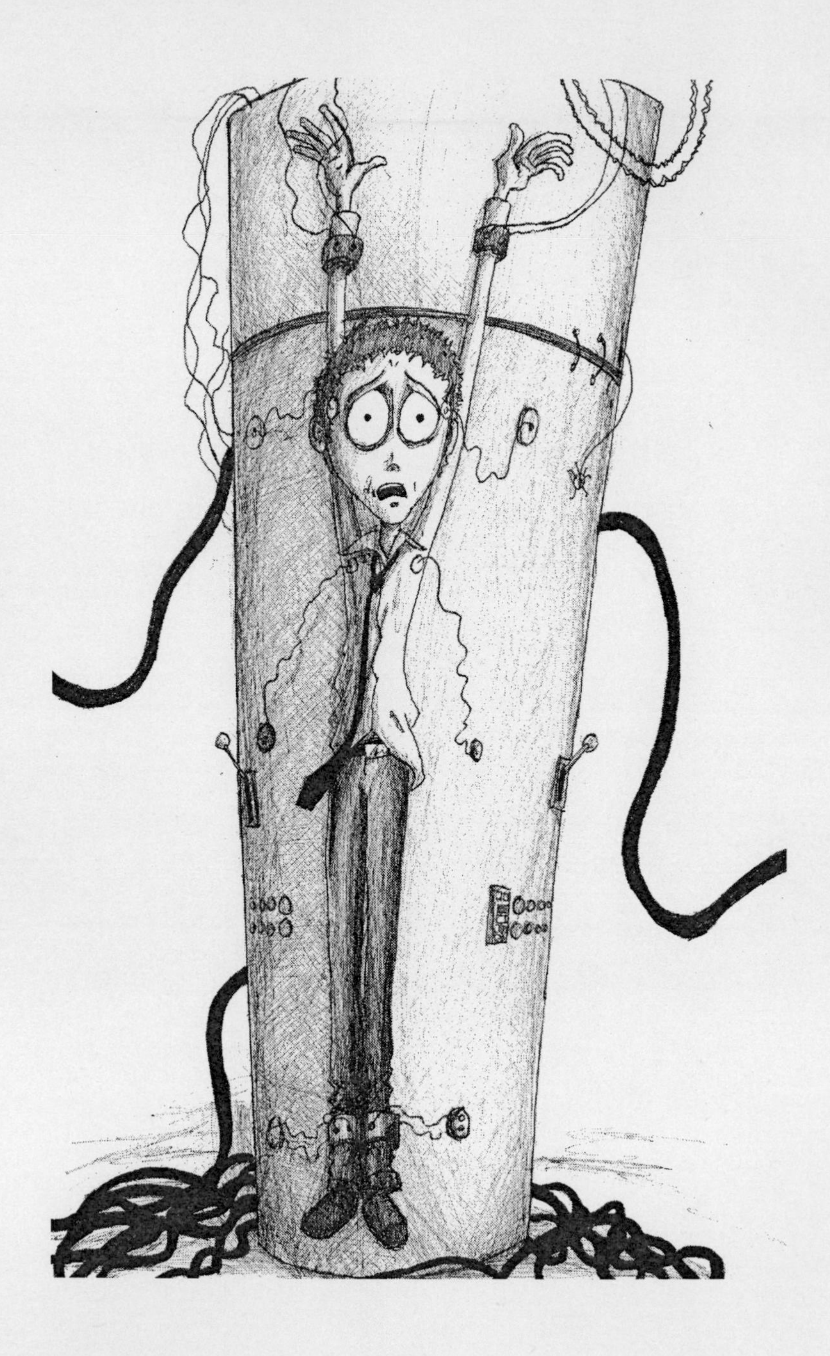

'Recycling what?' I asked.

'Luke, of course. See if we can make something useful out of him.'

'Danny, Will, thank goodness!' Luke shouted. 'Get me out of here. Call the police. Do something!'

The alien pulled a lever and Luke's hair stood on end.

'Arghh, stupid lizard's trying to electrocute me,' Luke yelled.

The alien grinned. 'Shocking, isn't it?'

'Let him go!' I cried.

'Yeah, pick on someone your own size,' shouted Will.

'Bravely spoken.' The alien laughed,

pulling out a deadly looking weapon. It was like a blaster from Star Wars only bigger.

He pointed it at Will and made him climb a ladder to the top of a diving board overlooking a large tank of thick yellow liquid. At the top, he tied his legs with what looked like a thick rubber band.

'You, Will, have the honour of helping me with my gravity tests.'

Will looked petrified. 'I'm . . . I'm afraid of heights.'

'Don't worry, the Kurian moon mud will break your fall.'

Will looked down at the yellow liquid in the tank below. 'What is that?'

'Kurian moon mud – it's a bit like your

stale custard. But nicer.' The alien shoved Will off the end and he plunged downwards into the custardy gunge. But no sooner had he disappeared into the tank, he came zooming back out again like he was bungee jumping. His face was green and he was spitting out the moon mud. It must've been disgusting.

Striding over, the alien grabbed the back of my neck. 'Over here, I know you're just bursting to help me too,' he said.

'What about Will?'

'Oh, he can hang around for a while.'

The alien pushed me over to the table full of glass containers and test tubes filled with coloured liquids. There was an awful smell coming from the containers that smoked a bit and my eyes began to water.

He sat me down and shoved a book under my nose. 'I know how much you like Science, boy, so you can get to work with the experiments in this book. And hurry up. I've loads to get through and time's running out. And don't bother trying to escape – there's nowhere to run to anyway. And you wouldn't want anything really terrible to happen to your friends just yet.'

I scratched my head. The writing must've been alien. 'I can't read this!'

Rummaging in his pocket, the alien took out the orb along with a strange silver, comb-like object. Setting the orb down, he ran the comb-like object down the printed page which instantly began changing into English before my eyes.

'Now get on with it. I have to start packing the ship.'

As he turned, I reached out and put my hand on the orb only to feel a slimy hand grab my arm. The alien gave me a frosty stare. 'Ah ah, shouldn't touch what doesn't belong to you.'

The alien began carrying boxes of stuff aboard the spaceship but was never out of sight long enough for us to escape.

'Where are you - ouch - going?' Luke shouted between zaps of electricity. 'Cause if you're going then you can let me go.' He was pale green and sweating like a pig, the life was being sucked out of him. I was sure he couldn't take much more.

'If you must know I'm returning to Kurimus V to hand in my recommendation.'

'Recommending what exactly?' I asked.

'That we return and colonise your planet Earth. Pity you didn't look after it very well, still it does have quite a lot to offer.'

'In case you haven't noticed, the Earth is already colonised - BY US!' I cried.

'And you'll come in very useful - in some way - I'm sure.'

'Useful but . . . '

The alien waved the vaporiser at me. 'Enough talk! Get on with your work! I want to be gone soon.'

There was a clanking noise as a huge rubber tube began descending, covering Luke's head. I figured it must be going to recycle Luke into goodness knows what. He began yelling, 'Help, he's killing me!'

My hands were trembling, spilling some of the chemicals I was pretending to do something with. They mixed together sending a burst of stinky steam up my nostrils - a stinky steam that suddenly gave me an idea.

Ignoring the book, I began mixing up all the chemicals, especially the nasty smoky ones. As I did, the mixture began to bubble and give off more and more smoke, which soon floated upwards, filling the air.

The alien noticed and yelled, 'What are you doing there; can't you follow a simple book?'

In a couple of minutes the entire hangar was full of thick smoke. You couldn't see a thing. I chose my moment and made a dash to roughly where Luke was. By crawling on all fours and keeping close to the ground, sort of beneath the smoke, I discovered you could see a bit.

'Stupid boy, are you trying to blow us all

up, boy . . . where are you?' I heard the alien ranting.

I blundered about, blinded and choking. I figured I had to be close to Luke but couldn't find him. The alien's growling seemed to be very close. At one point I imagined I could feel his hot breath on my neck, but it was a jet of hot steam.

A moment later I found Luke's ankles.

'What . . . who's that? Geroff you big slimeball!'

'SShh! It's me. We're getting out of here.'

'Get these stupid wires off me,' Luke moaned.

The cables fizzed as I touched them

and I felt my fingers crackle with static as I short-circuited the system.

I got him free and we both fumbled over to find Will.

Luckily I heard the alien fall over and scream something in alien language, which I'm sure wasn't very nice but it bought us some time.

Will was still hanging upside down.

'Will, over here - give me your hand,' Luke whispered from the edge of the gunge pool.

The smoke cleared for a moment and he saw us. He stretched out a hand over the gunge and Luke grabbed him, pulling him over.

Luke and I managed to free him then we ran to where I figured the door had to be. I was wrong.

'Boy, where are you? When I catch you I'm gonna see to it that you don't run anywhere again.' The alien threatened.

I scuttled sideways like a crab, groping the hangar wall with my palms.

'Don't be a fool, there's no escape!'

At last, I felt a door. I shoved the door bar and we all burst outside, stumbling frantically through the thick undergrowth.

We'd been running for a while when I yelled. 'Stop!'

Luke and Will stopped and looked round at me, panting hard. 'What?'

'We've got to go back.'

Luke stared at me like I'd gone mad.

'You're kidding, right?'

'You heard what he said; they're going to colonise the Earth. We have to think of a plan to stop him.'

'Let's go, Will.'

'Don't go back,' Will pleaded. 'He'll do something terrible to you.'

'Come on,' said Luke, 'if he wants to be stupid then let him.'

Luke and Will set off again. Will glanced back at me. 'Are you coming?'

I shook my head. I watched them

disappear into the undergrowth. And suddenly I was on my own, with the responsibility of saving the planet.

Time wasn't on my side so I hurried back through the rough countryside. Once the alien realised we'd escaped he'd probably just pack up and blast off.

Arriving back at the hangar, I found a window and peered inside. There was no sign of the alien. Maybe I was wrong he had gone to look for us after all. I couldn't sense him so I felt it should be safe enough. I entered the hangar. The hatch of the spaceship was open and, taking a deep breath, I went aboard.

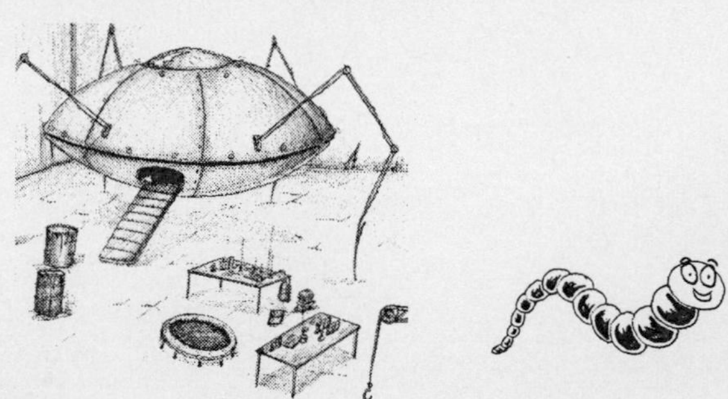

Inside the Alien Spaceship

Tuesday 4.55pm

A short corridor led to the main flight deck, a room with a single chair in front of a large window. There were loads of computers and instrument panels, all of which meant nothing to me. I quietly crept about wondering what I thought I could do. I noticed a small terminal near the corner, with four display screens showing different views of the solar system. A red dotted line cut through all the screens, plotting a route.

'The navigation computer, maybe . . . ' I mumbled aloud.

I stared at the line. I guessed it might be the alien's trajectory home to Kurimus V. I punched some keys on a keyboard then jumped as an alarm sounded in the flight deck and a panel of lights began flashing. I thumped the keyboard with my palms then breathed a sign of relief as the alarm fell silent.

Seconds later, I was sure I heard a noise like footsteps coming from outside.

There was no time to do anything clever but maybe if I *touched* the screens with both my hands something might happen. Maybe this computer wasn't entirely Danny proof. The dotted line began flashing, then

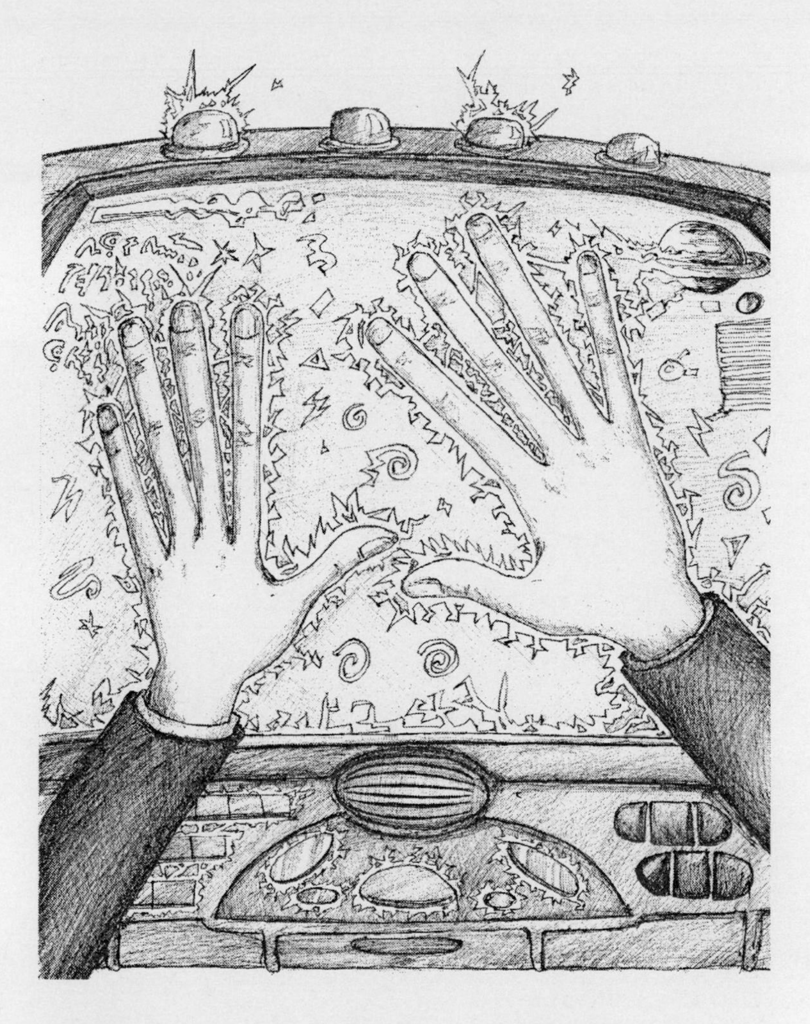

jumping around, following my fingers. Some alien language flashed up, like data or something. The line writhed round the screen in different directions like one of the coral snakes from Oli's pet shop.

More alien data streamed up the screen, getting faster and faster till it was a blur, then with a bleep, the four screens went blank. My heart skipped a beat. For a second I thought I'd disabled the whole ship, but the rest of the computers still seemed to be working.

I didn't know what I'd done but hopefully it was enough to displace the alien's journey home to deliver his recommendation. As I was about to leave, I spotted a green orb like the one the alien had spoken into on the Science Bus. I lifted one and put it in my pocket. Then more noises outside helped me decide to get out while I could.

I stopped at the hatch and looked around. My weird sense was tingling but I couldn't see anything. I ran out of the hangar and back outside after Luke and Will.

I hadn't got far when I stumbled on a fallen branch, falling to my knees. At the same time my weird sense suddenly pounded inside my head. I got to my feet only to feel someone grab the back of my neck.

Should've escaped while you could, boy. I'd have made sure you didn't remember anything about this little adventure.

What . . .

I looked up. It was the alien.

'Y . . . You're hurting me!' I cried.

You've wasted enough of my time. I felt the cold steel of the blaster press against the side of my head. *'Start walking!'*

I was conscious of the touch telepathy the alien was using and fought to keep my mind blank, especially after what I'd just done.

Why were you still snooping round anyway, what were you up to?

I clenched my teeth and started to name the planets of the solar system in my head starting with Mercury, anything to keep my mind from thinking about . . .

Think you're clever, don't you?

Then I imagined the alien dangling from the bungee rope back at the hangar.

Very funny, boy. You'll go down a storm back on Kurimus V. You're just the sort of specimen I need to take back.

I'm not going with you.

Oh but I think you'll find you've no choice.

I felt sick. Travelling halfway round the galaxy with an alien who had a sick sense of humour was not for me. Not to mention what he had planned for me once we got to Kurimus V. I had to escape. But I couldn't think about that. Not now.

We arrived at the hangar and he pushed me up the hatch of the spaceship. He'd let go of my neck now so I had a chance to think.

I noticed the floor of the spaceship had a strip of red carpet-like stuff down its middle. It gave me an idea. I shuffled my feet on it, trying not to make it too noticeable. I felt my arms tingling as the static electricity built up inside my body, trebled by my weird sense.

Waiting till I was fully charged, I stopped dead in my tracks and shouted. 'I'm not going with you - you can't make me!'

With a growl, the alien grabbed the back of my neck and as he did he got a huge electric shock that sent him flying backwards off his feet, dropping the vaporiser gun. I dashed past him but he rolled over and lunged at me, catching my foot.

'Stop, you little slime ball. I haven't time for this stupidity!'

I pulled my foot out of my shoe and ran on, and for a split second the name Cinderella flashed through my mind.

I ran through the door hatch, striking the door panel. The hatch started closing, but slowly. Slow enough for the alien to make a dive for the bottom gap. He fired the vaporiser, stunning my leg and I hobbled hopelessly for a few steps till he grabbed me.

The alien stuck the vaporiser in my back.

'Let the boy go!'

Both our heads spun round at the same time. Farmer Mudd stepped into the hangar holding the shiniest pitchfork I'd ever seen.

The alien grinned. 'Well, well - Grandpa to the rescue.'

Farmer Mudd bared his false teeth. 'That's Mr Mudd to you.'

'Ah, the mad farmer - I was reading about you.' The alien nodded to the pitchfork. 'Hardly a shotgun is it? I thought farmers were meant to have shotguns or did they take yours off you . . . ?'

'Still put more holes in ya than a pepper pot. So like I said, let the boy go an' nobody gets hurt.'

The alien roared with laughter. 'You really think I'm scared of a pathetic human creature like . . . '

Farmer Mudd suddenly lunged forward coolly swinging the pitchfork upwards in an almost ninja like move and knocking the vaporiser out of the alien's hand. It twirled high in the air. Stamping on his foot, I wriggled out of his grip and jumped, only just catching the vaporiser with my finger ends. I ran to stand beside Farmer Mudd.

'How'd you . . . ?

'Saw the smoke,' he said, neither of us taking our eyes off the alien who was crouched, rubbing his foot and glowering at us.

I pointed the vaporiser at him. 'Aren't you running late?'

'You're brainless!'

'You're beaten!'

The alien backed up to the hatch. 'This is pathetic. You're right; I'm not wasting another minute here. I'll deal with you both when WE come back. Then we'll see who's beaten.'

We stood watching as the alien climbed into the hatch and went inside. Then the low rumble of the spaceship's main engines filled the air.

The ship hovered over to the rusted hangar doors leading to the outside and crashed through them. Then it streaked off into the sky.

Farmer Mudd clapped me on the back and smiled. 'I think you've a lot to tell me on the ride home. I've got the tractor outside.'

Country Road

Tuesday 6.30pm

I bumped about in the back of Farmer Mudd's trailer, examining the vaporiser gun (another trophy to add to my secret weird collection, which included Martian rock and a piece of a landing beacon that fell off a flying saucer).

I had told Farmer Mudd everything. 'I knew I wasn't mad,' he said.

'I did too.'

Suddenly I heard a strange bleeping noise. The orb! I'd totally forgotten about it.

I took it out of my pocket and stared. It was glowing. There was a hissing noise like most radios make when I'm near them. But amazingly the next thing I heard was the alien's voice - crystal clear. He was yelling.

'Boy . . . come in, boy. What have you done you little moon worm? I know you can hear me. I'm hurtling through your solar system on a one way course to the edge of the universe. And all comms are down except this one. Seems someone's been fiddling with my ship - do you hear me, boy?'

I didn't know how to work the thing and I didn't know whether it would be Danny proof but I held it to my mouth. 'This is

Danny. I read you very loud and clear. About your orbiting our solar system - I'm thrilled. Now you've no excuse for not learning the proper order of planets, starting from the sun, first there's Mercury . . .'

'You think you're soooo clever, don't you?' he broke in. 'But you've forgotten I can contact my home planet and organise the invasion from . . . zzz . . . what's . . . wrong, malfunction brzzzp . . . smoke . . . orb . . . arghh you've ruined . . . everything!'

Then I remembered I'd touched the alien's orb back at the hangar when I was mixing up the chemicals before he snatched it off me. The orb began hissing again, drowning out his ranting and then the light suddenly went out. I rolled it around in my hand, grinning proudly. Seemed my visit to the helm of the spaceship had paid off. And when I got home I could open the orb to see what Kurimus V technology was like.

Farmer Mudd glanced back. 'What was all that about?' he shouted above the roar of the tractor.

'I don't think we need worry about an alien invasion,' I smiled.

'That's grand news. Hey! I think I see two lads on the road. Wouldn't be your friends would they?'

Trudging up the lane, were Luke and Will. They seemed to be arguing. We pulled up beside them and I leaned out of the trailer. 'Wanna lift?'

They both looked totally shocked to see me.

'Danny, what are you doing here?'

Will seemed bewildered. 'We don't even know what we are doing here.'

I held up the vaporiser. 'Someone had to sort out the alien.'

'What are you talking about?' said Luke.

They clambered aboard. 'You know - Mr Allen, the spaceship, the experiments,' I said. They stared at me like I was mad. 'You really don't know?'

'Last thing I remember is trying to nick a few batteries from the Science Bus,' shrugged Luke.

Will nodded. 'Next thing we're wandering through the countryside. What do you know about it? How'd we get out here?'

The alien must've used some powerful mind trick to make them forget what had happened back at the hangar. How and when I don't know. But why hadn't he used it on me? I guess once he had decided to take me back with him as a human specimen he wanted my mind exactly as it should be. I decided there was probably no point in trying to explain everything to Will and Luke. They'd never understand.

'It's a long story. And I think I'd like to get home.'

'Where'd you get the gun?' asked Luke. 'Can I see it?'

He took it from me and before I could stop him, fired it at some trees.

There was a loud blast and loads of smoke as a few branches rustled in the tree.

'Careful back there!' yelled Farmer Mudd, driving off.

I took the vaporiser off Luke. 'Eh, I'll look after that.' I pushed it firmly down into one of my pockets.

They both looked at me strangely for a minute. Will opened his mouth as if he was going to ask some more questions but then Luke suddenly said, 'Hey, you've got a mobile, haven't you? Lend us it - I need to phone my mum.'

'Oh no! Look at the time! So do I! My mum will kill me when I get back . . . ,' said Will.

I gave him the mobile and sat back, looking up at the sky. Venus was just about visible to the naked eye. I smiled, thinking about the alien. I wondered how he was enjoying the first orbit of his solar system sightseeing tour . . .

END OF FILE . . .

This is the end of the file but it's not The End. It's just one out of hundreds more weird files on the World Wide Weird Web. It wasn't even the end of Mr Allen, as I found out the day I stumbled on a horrible green finger half buried in the wet grass in a field at Mudd Farm . . . but that's another file . . .

Warning

Now you've read this file please do not just put it on your bookshelf or bedside table where other people might see it. Put it away safely. You've got to be careful it doesn't get into the wrong hands - I'm sure you can see why. If you have to lend it to a friend just be careful who you lend it to - even be careful who's reading it over your shoulder because they're out there - aliens, extra-terrestrials, whatever you want to call them. If you spot anything weird please let me know, you can find me on the World Wide Weird Web!

Also available in the Reluctant Reader Series from:

Sam's Spitfire Summer *(WW2 Adventure)*
Ian MacDonald ISBN 978 1 905637 43 0

Alien Teeth *(Humorous Science Fiction)*
Ian MacDonald ISBN 978 1 905637 32 2

Eyeball Soup *(Science Fiction)*
Ian MacDonald ISBN 978 1 904904 59 5

Chip McGraw *(Cowboy Mystery)*
Ian MacDonald ISBN 978 1 905637 08 9

Close Call *(Mystery - Interest age 12+)*
Sandra Glover ISBN 978 1 905 637 07 2

Beastly Things in the Barn *(Humorous)*
Sandra Glover ISBN 978 1 904904 96 0
www.sandraglover.co.uk

Cracking Up *(Humorous)*
Sandra Glover ISBN 978 1 904904 86 1

Deadline *(Adventure)*
Sandra Glover ISBN 978 1 904904 30 4

The Crash *(Mystery)*
Sandra Glover ISBN 978 1 905637 29 4

The Owlers *(Adventure)*
Stephanie Baudet ISBN 978 1 904904 87 8

The Curse of the Full Moon *(Mystery)*
Stephanie Baudet ISBN 978 1 904904 11 3

A Marrow Escape *(Adventure)*
Stephanie Baudet ISBN 1 900818 82 5

The Haunted Windmill *(Mystery)*
Margaret Nash ISBN 978 1 904904 22 9

Trevor's Trousers *(Humorous)*
David Webb ISBN 978 1 904904 19

The Library Ghost *(Mystery)*
David Webb ISBN 978 1 904374 66

Dinosaur Day *(Adventure)*
David Webb ISBN 978 1 904374 67 1

Grandma's Teeth *(Humorous)*
David Webb ISBN 978 1 905637 20 1

The Curse of the Pharaoh's Tomb
(Egyptian Adventure)
David Webb ISBN 978 1 905637 42 3

The Bears Bite Back *(Humorous)*
Derek Keilty ISBN 978 1 905637 36 2

The Mum Manager *(Humorous)*
Suzi Cresswell ISBN 978 1 905637 45 4

Snakes' Legs and Cows' Eggs *(Multicultural)*
Adam Bushnell ISBN 978 1 905637 21 8

Donkeys' Wings and Worms' Stings
(Multicultural)
Adam Bushnell ISBN 978 1 905637 50 8